PICKLE-
CHIFFON
PIE

by
Jolly Roger Bradfield

Purple House Press
KENTUCKY

Published by Purple House Press, PO Box 787, Cynthiana, KY 41031
Read about our classic children's books at www.PurpleHousePress.com and
learn more about the author at www.RogerBradfield.com

2 3 4 5 6 7 8 9 10

A long time ago there was a fat little king who ruled over the land as far as he could see in every direction. He was very wise, and his kingdom was a happy one.

His wife, the Queen, kept his castle spotless and saw that his robes were cleaned and pressed. She was a very good cook and made him a pickle-chiffon pie every day.

But everybody has problems.

The King had a daughter. Oh, she was very nice, and did whatever he asked her to—but she was also very beautiful, and every prince in the neighborhood wanted to marry her. Every day

they came to the palace with flowers and gifts
for her.

To be polite, she would ask them all to stay
for supper, and that meant there would be less
pickle-chiffon pie for the King.

That was his problem.

Finally one day the King decided that his daughter should marry one of the princes. Then, at least, there would be fewer people at the dinner table each night.

He called for the three nicest princes and told them that they would be put to a test...and that the winner could marry the Princess!

The first, Prince Musselbaum, was very strong and brave. The Princess liked him because he was tall and had wavy hair and freckles.

The second, Prince Wellred, was very smart. He could count up to six hundred and eighty-four...and he read books three inches thick.

The Princess liked him, too, because he read beautiful stories to her, and sometimes played music under her window at night.

The third, Prince Bernard, wasn't very strong or very handsome or very smart; but the Princess liked him best of all. She didn't really know *why* she liked him—perhaps it was because he had a big smile and a funny nose.

It's hard to tell about princesses.

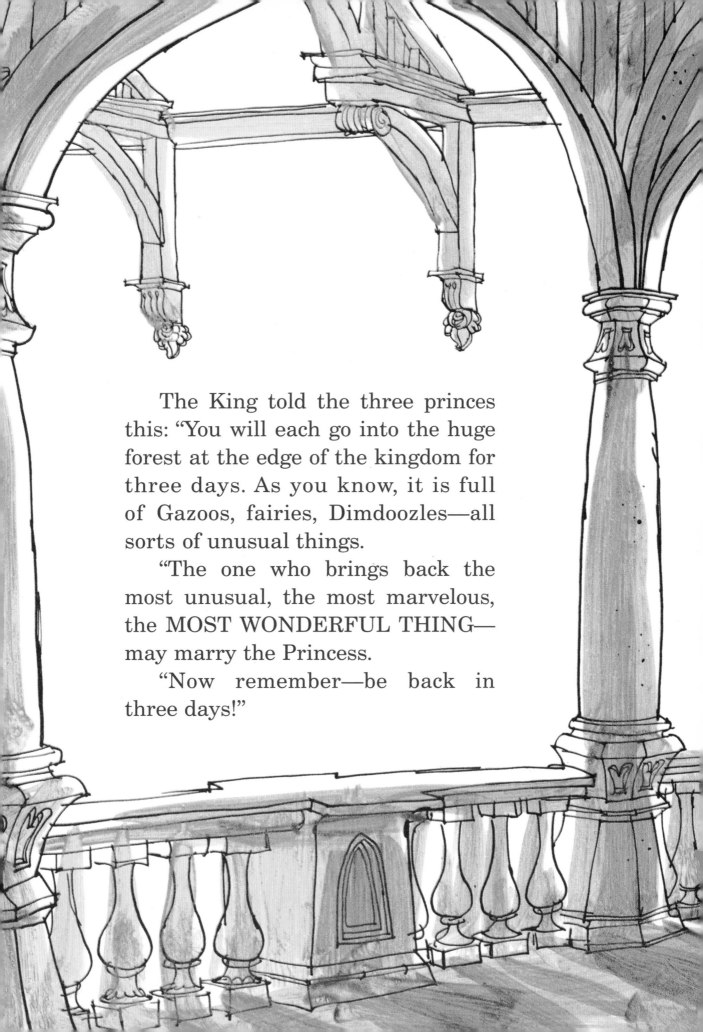

The King told the three princes this: "You will each go into the huge forest at the edge of the kingdom for three days. As you know, it is full of Gazoos, fairies, Dimdoozles—all sorts of unusual things.

"The one who brings back the most unusual, the most marvelous, the MOST WONDERFUL THING— may marry the Princess.

"Now remember—be back in three days!"

Musselbaum was delighted. Being stronger and braver than the others, he thought he would surely win. With a shout, he jumped onto his horse and galloped off in the direction of the forest.

At first he didn't see anything unusual...just a few small dragons, a troll peeking out of a tree, a medium-sized giant— the usual things one sees in a forest.

But finally, looking behind a huge boulder, he *did* see something different—a green and blue dragon with three heads, toasting marshmallows.

"Now *there's* something you don't see every day," thought Prince Musselbaum. "But I have two more days—I'll look a bit more."

On the second day he saw a Four-wheeled
Dimdoozle, with a pipe and wearing glasses.

"Now *there's* something different," thought
Musselbaum. "I've never seen a Dimdoozle
wearing glasses before! But I have one more
day—I'll look a bit more."

On the third day he saw something REALLY different—a huge lion juggling six cans of root-beer soup. He was wearing a velvet vest and roller skates.

"This must *surely* be the most wonderful thing in the whole forest!" cried Prince Mussel-baum. Bravely he grabbed the lion's tail and started dragging him back toward the castle.

M eanwhile, Prince Wellred was
searching, too.

The first day he spied a witch who could
turn people into frogs (which really wasn't so

special, except that she could do it with her eyes shut and one hand behind her back.)

"Now *there's* something you don't see every day," thought Wellred. "But I have two more days—I'll look a bit more."

On the second day he saw a Sixteen-footed
Gazoo that had a different kind of shoe on
each foot.

"Now *there's* something different," thought Wellred. "I've never seen a Gazoo with more than seven feet! But I have one more day left— I'll look a bit more."

On the third day he came upon something REALLY different—a giant with a green beard playing "Chopsticks" on two pianos.

"This must *surely* be the most wonderful thing in the forest!" cried Prince Wellred. "I've never heard *that* tune before!"

He cleverly told the giant what a fine piano player he was, and talked him into going back to the castle to play for the King.

N ow let's not forget Prince Bernard. He was searching, too.

On the first day he met an ogre so ugly that he scared the leaves right off the trees.

"Now *there's* something you don't see every day," thought Bernard. "But he might frighten the Princess if I brought him back. I have two more days—I'll look a bit more."

On the second day he discovered a tiny house tucked behind a tree. He peeked in and saw that it was filled with mice, all busily painting the most wonderful pictures!

"Now *there's* something different," thought Bernard. "But it really wouldn't be right to stop such happy, hard-working little fellows right in the middle of their work. I have one more day—I'll look a bit more."

On the third day he saw something REALLY different—a Three-nosed Snozzle with fuzzy ears and an orange polka-dot necktie. And it was busy making pickle-chiffon pie!

"This must *surely* be the most wonderful thing in the whole forest!" he cried. "I thought the Queen was the only one who could make pickle-chiffon pie! Oh, the King will be so happy!"

With that he grabbed the Snozzle's necktie and started leading it back toward the castle.

Prince Bernard had never been happier in his whole life.

It was hard work pulling the Three-nosed
Snozzle through the forest, but Prince Bernard
didn't mind; he was *sure* he would win the
contest to marry the Princess!

But he wasn't quite so happy when he saw

how sad the Snozzle looked.

"Don't feel bad," said Bernard. "You'll like living at the palace—it's much nicer than this dark old forest. And anyway, I *have* to take you back in order to marry the Princess."

Then Bernard noticed several tiny Snozzles peering out from behind the trees. "Why, aren't they cute!" he said. "Are—are they your children?"

The Three-nosed Snozzle nodded, with big, wet tears coming into its eyes.

"What will happen to them when you're gone? Do they have anyone to take care of them?"

The Snozzle shook its head sadly.

Prince Bernard sat down on a log to think. He thought of his love for the Princess. He thought of the Snozzle's love for its children.

For a long time it was very quiet and still in the forest.

Finally, with a sigh, the Prince let go of the Snozzle's necktie and watched it scamper off. Then he turned and walked slowly toward the castle.

His three days were up.

When all the princes were called to appear before the King, Musselbaum had a big smile on his face. He was sure he would win with his juggling lion. Wellred was smiling, too. He was just as sure that he would win when the King heard the giant play his two pianos!

Bernard hung his head sadly as he stood empty-handed behind the others.

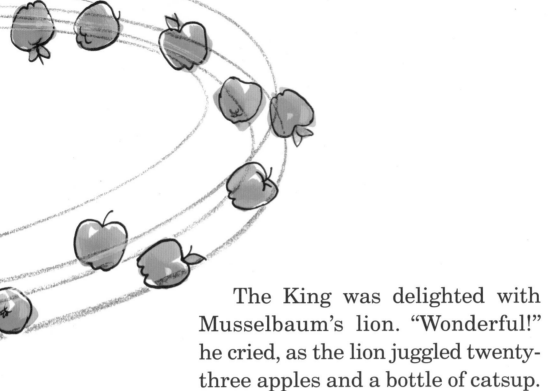

The King was delighted with Musselbaum's lion. "Wonderful!" he cried, as the lion juggled twenty-three apples and a bottle of catsup.

And when Wellred's giant played "Chopsticks" on his two pianos, the King laughed and clapped his hands in delight.

"How wonderful!" he cried. "So unusual!"

Then he turned to Bernard. "And what have you brought back?" he asked.

Prince Bernard bowed low before the King. He hoped that no one noticed the tears in his eyes as he raised his head and said softly, "Nothing, your Majesty."

He told of meeting the ugly ogre who might have frightened the Princess. He told of seeing the amazing mice whose painting he could not bring himself to interrupt. He told of the tiny Snozzle children that he could not bear to leave in the forest alone.

There was silence in the castle. No one spoke for a long time. Bernard wished that he could run and hide. Everyone was looking at him—all except the Princess and the Queen. They were whispering to the King.

The King nodded his head and smiled. "Bernard," he said in a loud voice, "*You* have won the right to marry the Princess!"

"But—but *why*, your Majesty? I didn't bring back *anything!*" said Bernard.

"Oh yes, you did, my son," said the King. "You brought back a story of kindness and love and consideration for others...truly THE MOST WONDERFUL THING OF ALL. You'll make a fine husband for my daughter!"

When Bernard married the Princess, Wellred's giant played the wedding march, and Musselbaum's lion put on a special exhibition to entertain the guests.

And guess who sent Bernard and the Princess the biggest pickle-chiffon pie anyone ever saw for a wedding present? That's right— the Three-nosed Snozzle with the fuzzy ears and the orange polka-dot tie.